KEY HUNTERS

THE
RISKY RESCUE

KEY HUNTERS

*Getting lost in a good book
has never been this dangerous!*

KEY HUNTERS

THE RISKY RESCUE

by Eric Luper

Illustrated by Lisa K. Weber

SCHOLASTIC INC.

For Eric K. and Robbie H. for forcing me to be creative, sometimes until four in the morning

Text copyright © 2018 by Eric Luper.
Illustrations by Lisa K. Weber, copyright © 2018 Scholastic Inc.

This book is being published simultaneously in hardcover by Scholastic Press.

All rights reserved. Published by Scholastic Inc., *Publishers since 1920.* SCHOLASTIC, SCHOLASTIC PRESS, and associated logos are trademarks and/or registered trademarks of Scholastic Inc.

The publisher does not have any control over and does not assume any responsibility for author or third-party websites or their content.

Library of Congress Cataloging-in-Publication Data available

ISBN 978-1-338-21229-7

10 9 8 7 6 5 4 3 2 1   18 19 20 21 22

Printed in the U.S.A.   40
First printing 2018

Book design by Mary Claire Cruz

CHAPTER 1

"Are you sure this is a good idea?" Cleo asked as she and Evan tiptoed into the school library. The lights were off, and early-morning sunlight streamed in around the edges of the window shades.

Evan shook a long black case he was carrying. "What I *am* sure about is if I lose my trombone when we go into our next adventure, I'm in big trouble."

"We're about to sneak into a secret,

magical library, slip into the pages of a dangerous book, and go on an exciting adventure. And you're worried about your trombone?" Cleo couldn't believe it.

"Do you know how much a new trombone costs?" Evan asked.

"No."

"More than you have in your piggy bank, I can tell you that."

"I have a soccer ball bank," Cleo said. "Piggy banks are for babies."

"Hey, *I* have a piggy bank. His name is Mr. Oinks."

Cleo chuckled. "You'll just have to leave your trombone behind."

"I don't have much choice," Evan said. "We have to get the four Jeweled Greats without Locke or he'll share whatever power finding them will give us. That could be dangerous."

To everyone else, George Locke was their mild-mannered school librarian. But Evan and Cleo knew better. The man was a greedy snake, determined to collect four priceless books that were hidden inside the stories in the magical library beneath their school—books that might give their finders mysterious powers.

Cleo scanned the dim library. "No sign of Locke here."

"Or his evil helpers, Glen and Gary," Evan added.

"The library sure looks different with the lights off, doesn't it?" Cleo said. "Almost as creepy as the magical library downstairs. That library seems to have a life of its own, sort of like it's watching us."

"Don't say that right before we have to go down there," Evan said. "You're freaking me out."

They crept through the maze of shelves to the farthest, darkest corner of the library.

Cleo gasped. "The secret bookcase is already open!"

She was right. The book called *Literature: Elements and Genre from Antiquity to Modern-Day* had been pulled out, and the heavy door had been shoved to the side. Cobwebs in the doorway swayed in a warm breeze.

Evan and Cleo glanced at each other in concern. They peered down the stairs. Orange light flickered from below.

"The fireplace is lit," Evan said. "Someone is down there."

They raced down the steps. The magical library was just as they had left it the day before. Soaring shelves were filled with books of all sizes and colors. Ledges and walkways wrapped around the huge room, accessible by ladders, slides, bridges, and spiral staircases. At the far end of the room, a fire crackled in the fireplace. Above that hung a huge tapestry that showed an image of an open book with people swirling into it amid a sea of colorful letters. On the left stood a glass case that held the Rubaiyat, a jeweled book Evan and Cleo had recovered on their last adventure. It was hard to believe it had been less than a day since they had gone on their *Titanic* voyage, but Evan still felt the chill of the North Atlantic waters.

The kids cautiously walked across the library and looked into the case. Next to the sparkling book were three empty pedestals.

"At least Locke didn't steal the Rubaiyat," Cleo whispered, running her hands along a shelf filled with heavy books. Each one was sealed with a small lock.

Evan looked past Cleo to a low desk along the wall. The book that sat on it caught his eye. It lay crookedly, which was strange in this perfectly organized library. But, even stranger, its pages were spread open. Evan knew that every book in this magical library was supposed to be locked.

"It looks like someone forced his way into this book."

Evan picked up the book and laid it on the table in front of Cleo. The cover was made of rough crocodile skin, and green vines grew around it. A warm breeze seemed to be coming from the book. *Did the pages just rustle a little?* Evan thought.

Cleo spun the book to face her. "What's the title?"

Evan peeked at the cover. "It's called *Quest for the Lost Sloth*."

"Sloths are so cute," Cleo said. "Maybe this will be a fun adventure!"

Evan doubted it, but it didn't make sense to disagree. Neither of them had any idea what was inside. It could be anything . . . in any place . . . at any time . . .

Evan smiled, thinking of all the possibilities a book had to offer. "The latch is broken," he said. "Locke forced it open somehow."

Cleo reached into her pocket and pulled out the brass key they'd gotten on their last adventure. It dangled from a chain. "Then what good is this?"

"No idea," Evan said. "But we should probably use it anyhow."

Cleo nodded and shut the book. "You should probably hide your trombone somewhere," she said. "I have a feeling we'll be zip, zap, zipping out of here soon."

Evan tucked his instrument under the table and crossed his fingers. If he lost that trombone, his parents would be furious. They'd probably take every penny out of Mr. Oinks to pay for it.

Cleo examined the lock. The brass latch was twisted, and the slot was squashed. She pressed the lock together the best she could. Then she thrust the key into the keyhole and turned.

Letters burst from the pages of the book like a thousand crazy spiders. The letters tumbled in the air around them and began to spell words. The words turned into sentences. The sentences turned into paragraphs. Before long, they could barely see through the letter confetti.

Then everything went black.

CHAPTER 2

It might have been the constant humming or the pressure in his ears, but the instant Evan opened his eyes, he knew they were on an airplane.

It was a small plane, not like the big jet he'd taken when he went to visit his Uncle Donnell in South Carolina. This plane only had about twenty seats. It also had no flight attendants to bring him juice and chocolate cookies.

His foot bumped against something heavy. His trombone was stowed under the seat. The black case shone like new. "Oh, great," he muttered.

"What's great?" Cleo asked.

Cleo was sitting across the aisle from him. She wore big sunglasses and a straw hat. A boy Evan had never seen before sat behind her. He was the only other passenger on the plane. The boy was wearing a shirt with pockets all over it and thick rubber hiking sandals. His arms were wrapped around a cardboard box that rested on his lap.

"Do you think we're going someplace warm?" Cleo asked Evan.

"What makes you say that?"

"Oh, just the vacation clothes we're wearing. Maybe we're going to Hawaii!"

Evan touched his hat and smiled. "After

freezing in the North Atlantic, I could use some warm weather."

"Hawaii?!?" The boy behind them laughed. "We're not going to Hawaii. We're headed to cold and windy Chicago."

Evan shivered.

The boy slid to the edge of his seat. "My name is Gabriel. I live here in Brazil, but I'm on my way to see my parents. They're both scientists at a university."

"Ooh, what kind of scientists?" Evan asked.

"My father is an anthropologist and my mother is a zoologist," Gabriel said.

"A zoologist?" Cleo said. "She studies zoos?"

"Animals, actually," Gabriel said. "And anthropologists study human culture. They made a discovery and had to rush back to the university to report it." Gabriel leaned in even closer and whispered: "Something about what's inside this box."

"What is it?" Cleo asked.

Gabriel shrugged. "It's top secret."

"I don't mean to be rude, but how top secret could it be if they let their ten-year-old son carry it around?" Evan asked.

"First of all, I'm eleven. And second, I have this tracking device." Gabriel pulled out a small gadget that looked like a thick smart-phone. On the screen, a blinking arrow pointed right at the box. "The GPS will always tell me where to go."

Cleo winked at Evan. "I'm sure you're very responsible," she said, "but if you were my kid, I'd tell you that box is top secret and fill it with stuffed animals just to make you feel like you were doing something important. That way, you'd follow directions better."

Gabriel's eyebrows pushed together. "I do plenty of important things for my parents. I keep the research camp clean. I fetch fresh water from the well. I organize the canned food—"

"Oh, organizing food," Cleo said. "That sounds very important."

"Well, if you don't believe me, I'll open the box right now."

Cleo smiled. "If you say so."

Gabriel ran his fingers along the edge of the box until he found a flap. He tugged at the cardboard and tore the tape. Shredded newspaper spilled out. Gabriel reached in and pulled out a note. He unfolded it and read it aloud:

dearest gabriel,

if you are reading this note, we fear the worst. above all, get yourself to safety. be sure to keep the Contents of this bOx safe, though. you will need it. we're sorry we coulDn't spEnd YOUR BIRTHDAY with you, but we'll be sure to have cupcakes when you get to us.

with love,

mãe e pai

"Who are Mãe e Pai?" Cleo asked.

"Those words mean mother and father in Portuguese."

Gabriel stuffed the letter into one of his shirt pockets and reached deeper into the box. He smiled and pulled out a golden statue. It was the size and shape of a coconut and had a cute, shining face that smiled up at them. The statue's arms wrapped around its body as though it was hugging itself with its long claws.

Evan leaned in closer. "Is . . . Is that a . . . ?"

"It's a statue of a sloth," Cleo said. "A cute golden sloth! Sloths are my favorite animal!"

Gabriel turned the statue over in his hands. A small black box was attached to its side. A red light on it blinked every few seconds.

Evan figured that must be the tracking device.

"Sloths are my favorite, too," Gabriel said.

"Do your parents study them?" Evan asked.

"No, they found clues that might lead them to secret caves deep in the Amazon where ancient humans once lived. They are trying to figure out when man first came to South America."

"And woman," Cleo added.

Gabriel nodded. "And woman."

"What does that have to do with sloths?" Evan asked.

"I don't know," Gabriel said. "But they discovered something so important they had to rush back to Chicago to tell people about it."

"It seems strange to rush around over something that happened thousands of years ago," Cleo said.

"That's how science is," Gabriel explained. "The first one to announce a discovery is the one who gets credit for it. It could be big for their careers."

"A sloth can be big for someone's career?" Cleo asked.

Gabriel shrugged.

Just then, the plane shook and began to dive.

CHAPTER 3

"What's going on?" Evan hollered. His body jerked forward against his seat belt.

The plane tilted to the side, and Cleo clutched the armrests. The golden statue tumbled into the aisle and rolled to the front of the plane. Gabriel dove after it.

The door to the cockpit swung open, and a familiar-looking pilot walked out.

"Locke!" Evan and Cleo gasped.

Locke stepped over Gabriel. He was

wearing an airline pilot's jacket and hat. His mirrored sunglasses glinted as bright as his teeth, which they could see behind his evil sneer. "I thought I would beat you into this story by coming in early."

"You weren't early enough," Cleo whispered angrily.

"Let me tell you how this story goes. You give me that statue and go down with the plane," Locke said. "I'm the hero of this adventure."

The plane tilted the other way. Gabriel cried out as he and the statue tumbled around. He still clutched the tracking device in his hand.

"No hero would send an airplane crashing into the jungles of Brazil," Evan said.

"Brazil, Guyana, Suriname, who knows?" Locke said. "There's a lot of rain forest down there. But you won't have to worry about the

20

dangers of the jungle." He pointed over his shoulder at a bulky backpack with lots of straps. "There is one parachute."

Locke flung open the door. His pilot's hat flew out into the open sky. Wind whipped into the plane, sending papers, comfy pillows, and anything else not fastened down swirling around. The plane tilted again, and Gabriel and the statue tumbled toward the open door. Gabriel grabbed a flapping seat belt, but the rest of him rolled out the door. His body thumped against the outside of the plane.

"Gabriel!" Cleo screamed. She unhooked her seat belt and dove toward him. At the last second, Cleo grabbed Gabriel by one of his shirt pockets. He grunted and reached for the statue with his free hand, but it slipped through his grasp and fell out of the plane into the open sky.

"My statue!" Gabriel and Locke cried out at the same time.

Locke struggled toward the door, while Evan unbuckled his seat belt and made his way to the front. Evan had to get that parachute. None of them knew how to land a plane!

Locke snatched the tracker from Gabriel and moved to the edge of the door, ready to leap out. The wind flattened his hair to his head.

Evan ran forward and leaped at Locke, but Locke was too quick. He spun around and kicked Evan with a heavy boot. The knobby treads thumped Evan in the chest, and he fell back against the first row of seats.

"Have fun landing the plane!" Locke said. "I've got the tracker, and I've got the parachute!" And with that, Locke jumped out of

the plane. He tumbled around a few times and then spread his arms wide. Within seconds, a yellow parachute with purple polka dots ballooned open, and he floated away.

"Why couldn't your parents discover a square statue?" Evan called to Gabriel. "They don't roll as easily."

"Next time I see a prehistoric man I'll be sure to let him know," Gabriel said. "What do we do now?"

Cleo pulled Gabriel into the plane and struggled to her feet. "We have to land this plane!"

"You guys buckle in and prepare for a crash landing," Evan said. "I'll go up to the cockpit and try to figure something out."

"What do you know about flying airplanes?" Cleo said.

"I played an airplane game on my

computer once," Evan said. "It was called *Danny Runway: Flying Ace.*"

Cleo shrugged. "That's more than me. Go for it."

Evan stumbled to the cockpit. There were way more buttons and lights than he had ever seen before—way more than Danny Ace had probably ever seen before. A beeping sound blared from a speaker.

Evan slid into the seat on the left, buckled himself in, and put on a set of heavy headphones. He looked out the window. There was jungle as far as he could see. "Mayday! Mayday!" he yelled. No one responded.

He grabbed the controls and pulled back. They wouldn't budge.

He pulled harder and called over his shoulder, "Cleo! I need your help!"

Cleo made her way into the cockpit and

buckled herself into the copilot's seat. She grabbed the controls, and together they pulled as hard as they could. The sticks slowly eased back, and the nose of the plane began to lift.

"We're leveling out!" Evan said.

"Now what?" Cleo asked.

Evan looked around at the panels in front of him. He found the fuel gauge. An orange light was blinking below it. The arrow was pointing to E. "The fuel tank is empty!"

"I guess we won't be flying to Hawaii *or* Chicago," Cleo said. "Let's just get this thing on the ground."

Evan turned the steering wheel. The plane veered right. He pushed forward and back. The plane dipped and rose. It felt like he was flying in a giant, super-heavy glider. The problem was that this glider was going to crash soon.

"I'm going to pull up at the last minute and land the plane belly first," Evan said. "If we don't smash straight into a tree, we may survive."

"You don't sound too confident," Cleo said.

"I'm not." Evan looked at the jungle ahead. A muddy brown stripe snaked through the greenery. Light sparkled on the surface. Water. "We'll come in close to the river. The trees look smaller there."

"You still don't sound too confident," Cleo said.

"And you don't sound very supportive. Now help me with the controls."

Both kids grabbed their wheels and pulled back gently. The nose of the plane lifted up, and they began to sink toward the jungle. Evan watched a dial that showed the wings of the plane to make sure they were as level as possible. He turned slightly to follow the curve of the river. Soon, the uppermost branches of the jungle flicked at the bottom of the plane.

"Are you sure about this?" Cleo asked as heavier branches began to hit the plane.

Evan pulled back on the controls some more. Cleo did the same. The plane shook and jolted as they slammed into something on their way down. Gabriel yelped from behind them. Metal screeched as the wings tore away. The plane bucked hard. Evan could only watch as they hurtled closer and closer toward the jungle floor.

"Am I sure we're doing the right thing?" He glanced at Cleo. "Not at all."

CHAPTER 4

Evan's eyes were shut, and his head throbbed. The plane was still. The air was warm and damp. Bugs chirped and birds squawked. A warm breeze tickled his cheeks.

"I'll have a frozen limeade, please," he mumbled.

"Uh . . . Evan . . ." It was Cleo's voice. "I don't think there are any limeades around here."

"It's so hot . . . My mouth is dry. I want a frozen limeade."

"Evan." Cleo's voice sounded tense. "Open your eyes."

Evan opened his eyes.

They were still buckled into their seats. The wings and tail of the airplane were gone. The windows were shattered, and a huge gash had been torn in the fuselage. Also, they were hanging fifty feet in the air. Upside down.

Evan gasped. "What's going on?"

"The jungle vines caught us. We're hanging in a tree, but we could fall any second."

"Is Gabriel . . . ?"

"I'm okay," Gabriel called out. "This seat belt should win an award."

Metal creaked, and the airplane lurched.

"We've got to get out of this tree." Cleo unbuckled her harness. She dropped to the ceiling and rolled to her knees.

The plane lurched again.

Cleo moved more cautiously. She leaned out the shattered window and looked around. "There are vines and branches everywhere," she said. "We could climb down and . . ."

A tree branch cracked, and several vines snapped.

"No time to make a plan," Gabriel said, crawling into the cockpit. "Let's get out of here."

He pushed past Evan and Cleo and climbed out the window. Then he grabbed a hanging vine and swung to a nearby branch.

"Is he a gymnast?" Evan asked Cleo.

"I guess it's something you learn growing up in the jungles of Brazil."

"It's something you learn on the jungle gym at recess—or when you're about to fall fifty feet out of a tree," Gabriel said. "I'm pretty sure these branches weren't made to hold giant airplanes."

Evan knew Gabriel was right, and from the groaning of the branches he also knew if he didn't get out of the airplane soon he'd be going on another ride—straight down. He unbuckled his seat belt and climbed to the window. The closest vines and branches seemed too far away to reach—and the ground was about a million miles below— but what choice did he have?

"I liked it better when my eyes were closed," Evan said.

"Just jump," Cleo said.

So he did. Evan stretched out his arms and grasped the first thing he touched: a slim branch. It made a crackling sound, but it didn't break.

Evan worked his way from branch to branch until he could pull himself against the trunk. The cool moss wasn't as refreshing as a frozen limeade, but at least he felt safer than he had in that airplane.

SNAP! CRACK!! SNAP!!!

A huge vine broke, and the airplane began to fall.

Cleo squealed. She dove through the window, leaping to a different tree. She grabbed a branch just as the airplane dropped, cockpit first. It smashed on the ground and rolled over onto its side.

"That was a close call," Gabriel said.

"Oh, we've had closer," Cleo replied.

"Do you guys survive airplane crashes often?" Gabriel asked.

"Only when we're not curing werewolves or fighting dragons," she said.

"You're joking, right?"

"Yes," Evan said, glaring at Cleo. "My friend has a weird sense of humor."

Evan, Cleo, and Gabriel shimmied to the jungle floor.

They stood in a clearing covered with low ferns and dead leaves. The air seemed even stuffier than before. Bugs buzzed around them. Birds fluttered in the branches. Tree roots snaked across the ground like giant lizard tails. Nearby, a really wide, brown river flowed.

It was then Evan noticed his clothes were in tatters. His shirt and pants were torn, and

36

he was missing a shoe. Cleo looked just as bad. Grease was smudged across her cheek, and one sleeve was torn up to her shoulder.

"Watch out for brightly colored frogs," Evan warned. "Yellow, red—even blue."

"Why?" Cleo asked. "Will they attack us with sticky fingers and tongues?"

"No, I did a project on poison dart frogs last month. They live in the Amazon and are incredibly poisonous. Don't you remember?"

"Sorry. I don't remember that at all." Cleo marched over to what was left of the plane. It was nothing more than a dented metal tube with a door. "I've seen almost every episode of *Grizzly Romper: Survive in the Wild*," she said. "We need SH-WA-FI-FOO."

"Who's Shwafifoo?" Evan asked, dusting himself off.

"It's not a who, it's a what," Cleo explained.

"SH-WA-FI-FOO stands for Shelter, Water, Fire, and Food. We need all four if we want to survive." Gabriel grinned at Cleo. "I watch *Grizzly Romper*, too."

Cleo smiled back.

"We need to get out of here if we want to survive," Evan said, swatting a bug that was snacking on his neck.

"But first, we need to find the Golden Sloth," Gabriel said. "My parents' careers depend on it. Plus, they trusted me to take care of it."

Evan glanced at Cleo. They both knew they needed to find the statue, too. They had been inside enough books in the magical library to know they had to solve the challenge in each story in order to find a magical key to get back out. Finding the key usually meant going along with the book's crazy story line. They also knew they needed to find the second Jeweled Great before Locke. Who knew what powers he'd have at his fingertips if he got his hands on such an important treasure.

"Which way do we go?" Cleo asked.

"The statue fell out of the plane first," Gabriel said. "Then the pilot jumped out."

Evan looked up at the nearest tree and pointed through the jungle along a wide strip of broken branches. "Our plane came from that way," he offered. "If we head the way we came, we'll find Locke and the tracking device first, and then the statue."

"What are the chances we'll find one man

in this huge jungle?" Gabriel asked. "He must be miles away. And he might not stay in one place."

Cleo patted Gabriel on the shoulder. "We just need to figure out how to cover a long distance quickly."

Evan climbed atop a fallen log that slanted across the clearing. "What about the river?"

Cleo climbed beside him. "It looks as though it's going in the right direction."

"You want to build a raft and float down the Amazon?" Gabriel asked.

"A raft," Cleo said. "Great idea!"

"The Amazon River is one of the most dangerous places in the world," Gabriel explained. "Every creature that swims in it is deadlier than the last!"

"It can't be any more dangerous than camping out here and going nowhere," Evan said.

"Anyhow, you said it yourself," Cleo added. "We need to find that statue."

"I'll gather some thick branches for the base," Evan said.

Gabriel thought about it and nodded. "I'll collect some long vines to tie the raft together."

The boys began gathering materials, while Cleo searched inside the wrecked plane for anything they could use.

"Hey, I found your trombone!" Cleo tossed it out the door. The case had a dent in it and the corners were scuffed, but when Evan opened it, the instrument seemed all right.

"What about seat cushions?" Cleo asked, coming out into the sunlight. She held up a gray foam pillow.

"We're not building a sofa," Evan said,

dropping an armload of branches in the clearing.

With her free hand, Cleo held up a booklet from the plane's seat pocket. "Airplane seat cushions float, silly. If we tie them under the raft, we won't sink."

Evan's face got hot. He should have remembered that, but he and Gabriel were hard at work tying together the branches. Gabriel held the wood in place while Evan twisted the vines around them. Cleo began tying the seat cushions to the wooden frame. When they finished, the platform they had built was bigger than a door. They had even found an extra-long stick to help push them along if the water slowed down or if the raft got caught on something.

Gabriel patted Evan on the back. "I'm not sure it's seaworthy, but it's worth a shot."

Cleo wiped her hands on her pants. "It's our *only* shot. Let's drag it to the river and see if it floats."

Just then a low growl rumbled from somewhere in the thick bushes beyond the clearing.

Evan, Cleo, and Gabriel shrank back.

"I don't think we're alone," Evan said.

CHAPTER 5

A small creature with long arms crept from the bushes. It had grayish-brown fur and three long claws at the end of each paw. The creature seemed to be smiling like a happy old man.

Cleo kneeled. "Who are you, little guy?"

"It's a sloth," Gabriel said. "But they usually live high in the branches."

The sloth looked up at Cleo. Its eyes had

dark patches around them, like a raccoon's. The sloth smiled wider. "Urrr," it said.

"You're so cute," Cleo said, scratching his head. "I'm going to name you Teddy."

"I'm not sure it's a good idea to touch strange animals," Evan said.

"He's not strange," Cleo said. "He's Teddy." She picked Teddy up. He wrapped his long arms around Cleo's shoulders and hugged her tight. He was soft, warm, and very snuggly.

Suddenly, two other dark creatures swung through the trees toward them. They came fast, using their hands, feet, and long furry tails. Each had a large mane of black fur ringed with white around its face and a mouth that gaped open wider than a toilet seat.

"Howler monkeys!" Gabriel said. "That must be why Teddy isn't in his tree."

EVVVVVVV-NNNNNN!
CLEEEEEEEE-YO-YO-YO!!
KEEEEEE-EEEEEEYYYYY!!!

"Did they just say our names?" Cleo whispered.

"And 'key'?" Evan looked more closely at the monkeys. "I think that might be Locke's assistants, Glen and Gary."

"It can't b—" Cleo stopped when she realized Evan was right. Their eyes were dull, and they both wore the twisted grins she had seen so many times before.

But just as quickly as the howler monkeys had appeared, they vanished into the thick jungle. Their hooting and barking echoed through the branches.

"Where'd they go?" Cleo asked. Teddy hugged her tighter and buried his face in her shoulder.

"This is not a good sign," Gabriel said. "Howler monkeys are territorial. The only thing that would scare them away is another animal, a stronger one."

"Urrr," Teddy said.

"I doubt it was you," Gabriel said to Teddy. "No offense."

Just then something rustled through the tall grass. Its smooth body was colored in mixed patches of gray and green, with black spots running down the length of it. As it moved—slithered, even—glistening scales caught the light. When its head slid from the grass, two glowing yellow eyes stared at them.

"A giant snake!" Evan screamed.

"Urrr," Teddy said.

"It's an anaconda," Gabriel said. "That's the biggest snake in the world. Some get so large they can swallow a whole cow in one gulp."

"This one looks like it could swallow three!" Cleo grabbed one end of the raft. "Let's get to the river."

Evan set his trombone on the raft, and he and Gabriel took the other end. They slid the raft a few feet forward.

"We could have built this thing a little closer to the water," Cleo grunted.

"I'll try to remember that next time we're stranded in the Amazon," Evan said.

The anaconda slithered toward them. It was so thick that Evan wasn't sure he could get his arms around the fattest part of its body—not that he would care to try. They heaved the raft harder and got it to the river-bank before any of them became snake lunch. Gabriel was panting. Cleo wiped a trickle of sweat from her forehead. Teddy glanced at the anaconda and buried his face in Cleo's hair.

With one more shove, they pushed the raft into the river. Its front sank below the surface of the brown water. The vines that held the raft together made a stretching sound, but

Evan's knots held. Finally, the raft floated back up and bobbed a few times.

"Do you think it can hold all three of us?" Gabriel asked.

"All four of us," Cleo said. "Don't forget Teddy."

The anaconda hissed and began to coil up. It looked hungry.

"Only one way to find out," Evan said, pulling himself onto the rough wood next to his trombone. "It feels strong. Hop on."

Cleo and Gabriel climbed onto the raft, and Gabriel used the stick to push off from the shore. As they glided away on the quiet river, the anaconda hissed and disappeared into the tall grass.

The sun beat down on them. But as hot as it was, at least the river was quiet. It was also brown. Some parts reminded Cleo of melted chocolate—like in that movie about the kid in the chocolate factory—but she knew better than to drink any. Grizzly Romper always said river water was filled with germs. They took turns pushing the raft along. It was hard work. The bottom of the river felt muddy, and their stick got stuck with each push.

"Now I could *really* use a frozen limeade," Evan said.

"Don't talk about limeade," Gabriel said. "You're making me more thirsty."

"Is it 'more thirsty' or 'thirstier'?" Cleo asked.

"I'm so thirsty, I'd use both," Evan said. "More thirstier."

They drifted awhile longer. The river bent and looped so many times they weren't sure if they were even headed in the right direction anymore.

Evan took the stick from Gabriel and began to push. He felt proud that he, Cleo, and Gabriel had built this raft. It had taken them more than an hour, but now they were floating down the Amazon River on something they had built themselves. Even his trombone case was dry. The brass hinges gleamed in the sun.

Evan rocked the raft with his feet. Then, from the corner of his eye, he spotted a small ripple wiggling across the water. A moment later, he saw a few more ripples. Was a rock poking up from the riverbed? He looked more closely. The "rock" was black, shiny, and bumpy. It seemed to be drifting along behind them.

"Rocks don't move," Evan said, pushing more quickly. "Guys, I think we need to speed up a bit."

Cleo and Gabriel looked to where Evan was pointing, but the water had gone still again. The rock was gone.

"I think your mind is playing tricks on you, my friend," Gabriel said. "This heat—"

"I know what I saw," Evan said. "Something is following us."

"Maybe it's them," Gabriel said. Two howler monkeys with rings of white fur around their faces hung from a tree along the shore. The darker one opened his mouth wide and bellowed: **DAAAAYYYYYY—GRRRR!** The other monkey (Evan wasn't sure which was Glen and which was Gary) threw sticks and rocks, all of which fell short, splashing into the dark water.

"They're just taunting us," Cleo said. "Ignore them."

But Evan knew he had seen something. He

pushed the raft along and kept glancing back at the water behind them. The water didn't ripple again. The moving rock was nowhere to be seen. Glen and Gary, however, kept hooting and throwing stones.

DAAAAYYYYYY—GRRRR!

DAAAAYYYYYYN—GRRRR!!

JURRRR! JURRRR!! JURRRR!!!

The river turned, and Evan tried to keep the raft as close to the middle as he could. Something about the shallow weeds made him nervous. But who was he kidding? Everything about the Amazon made him nervous!

The river made another sharp turn, almost doubling back on itself. And that's when he saw it.

The long stick slipped from his hands. "Uhhh, guys . . ."

Cleo and Gabriel followed Evan's gaze.

A huge black lizard broke the surface of the water. It fixed its yellow eyes on the raft, crossed the small bit of muddy land toward them, and slipped back into the water.

"An alligator!" Cleo yelped.

"Urrr," Teddy grunted.

"It's a black caiman," Gabriel said. "King of the Amazon. That one's got to be twenty feet long."

"Where's our pushing stick?" Cleo asked.

"I dropped it in the water when I saw the caiman," Evan said.

Cleo sighed in frustration. "Now what are we supposed to do?"

"Urrr," Teddy said.

Gabriel dipped his hand into the water. "It feels like the river is running more quickly," he said. "Maybe we'll drift far enough along that the caiman won't follow us."

The raft floated a little farther down the river. The current sped up and pushed them along even faster. Evan and Cleo sat down. Gabriel kneeled.

"Is anyone else starting to get hungry?" Cleo asked. "I could really go for some mac and cheese."

"I want a hot dog," Evan said.

"Let's not talk about lunch," Gabriel said.

Suddenly, the caiman burst from the dark water, opened its giant jaws, and bit down on the raft. It clearly wasn't hungry for mac and cheese *or* a hot dog. It was hungry for Evan, Cleo, Gabriel, and Teddy!

CHAPTER 6

CRUNCH!!!

The caiman's huge teeth glistened in the sun as its jaws snapped shut. Wood splintered. Foam cushions tore apart. Evan, Cleo, Gabriel, and Teddy plunged into the murky water. Evan's trombone tumbled in beside them. The caiman thrashed around, its thick tail slamming into Evan's stomach.

"Urrr," Teddy said, grasping at Cleo.

Evan couldn't think of anything better to

say than "Urrr," either. His stomach hurt so much, he didn't bother to try. He kicked away and began to swim. Something drifted past him, and he grabbed it. It was his trombone case. And it floated! He pulled it to his chest and kept swimming.

Cleo grabbed one of the torn flotation cushions and swam alongside Evan. She paddled her arms and kicked her feet. Teddy climbed onto Cleo's shoulders and held on tightly to her neck. Something moved behind them. Cleo chanced a peek back. The caiman was just a few feet away and coming right toward them. Its giant jaws hinged open as it surged forward.

Evan had no choice. He lifted his trombone case and slammed it into the caiman's open mouth.

CHOMP! CHOMP!! CHOMP!!!

The caiman's teeth poked holes in the sides of the case. One of the brass buckles popped open. The caiman thrashed its head to the side and flung the trombone case away. Then the beast flicked its tail and came right at them again.

"Swim faster!" Gabriel yelled.

"Don't you think we're trying to do that?" Cleo said.

Teddy hugged Cleo tighter.

"I'm sorry," Cleo said, "but hugs won't be enough to stop a twenty-foot-long hungry black caiman."

Something brushed past Evan's leg—something big. Suddenly, the giant anaconda burst from the water and dove at the caiman. The caiman snapped at the snake, but the anaconda was too quick. It wrapped its body around the caiman, and the two began tumbling around. The anaconda squeezed, and the caiman hissed.

Evan would have loved to watch the caiman and anaconda battle if he were cozy on his couch watching a nature show. But he wasn't. He was neck-deep in the Amazon River right next to these wild animals! He grabbed his trombone case (at least what was left of it). Then he and Cleo swam toward Gabriel.

By the time they reached him, they were out of breath.

"I guess a hug *is* enough to stop a twenty-foot-long hungry caiman," Cleo panted. "What do we do now?"

"Keep swimming, I guess," Evan said.

"We should get out of the water," Gabriel suggested.

"Let's just go a little farther," Evan said. "The current seems quicker here."

"But the river is dangerous," Gabriel said.

"Everything is dangerous!" Evan and Cleo said at once.

As they floated downstream, the current got even faster.

Suddenly, the two howler monkeys appeared on the shore, barking and screaming like before.

"What are those crazy monkeys trying to tell us?" Cleo asked.

"Maybe they've never seen three kids in tattered clothes floating down the river with a sloth," Evan offered.

"I'm pretty sure that's true," Cleo said, "but I feel like they're trying to tell us something more."

"Uh, guys . . ." Gabriel arched out of the water and looked downstream. "Do you hear something?"

Evan heard a faint rushing sound. He looked downstream and saw white ripples ahead.

"It's white water," Gabriel said. "That means rocks and rapids. Very dangerous. Like I said, we need to get out of the river."

They swam toward shore, but the current was pulling too swiftly.

"I can't get over there!" Cleo said.

Evan paddled as hard as he could. "Me neither!"

"Pull your cushion to your chest and point your feet forward, like you're in a sitting position," Gabriel said over the roar of the river. "It's the safest way to go through the rapids!"

"You have to know an awful lot to live in the Amazon Jungle," Cleo said.

"I saw it on episode seven of season three of *Grizzly Romper: Survive in the Wild*," Gabriel said.

Evan looped his arm through the strap of the trombone case and hugged it as tightly as he could. Cleo turned around and pointed her feet downstream as Gabriel had suggested. Teddy's tiny claws dug into her back.

They went down a few narrow chutes where water sprayed high into the air. Evan had to push off several large boulders to keep from slamming into them. Cleo and Teddy squealed. After a few more chutes, the river widened again.

"Does the shoreline ahead of us look strange?" Gabriel asked.

Evan looked. "The trees . . . They just sort of . . ."

"They just sort of stop," Cleo said. "It's as though the river just ends."

"The Amazon River doesn't just end," Gabriel said. "It flows into the Atlantic Ocean."

"Well, it's doing something funky up there," Evan said.

The water began to ripple. Before anyone knew what was happening, Evan, Cleo, Gabriel, and Teddy tumbled over the edge of a giant waterfall.

Evan heard someone scream and slowly realized it was his own voice. He felt as though he was falling for miles. Below him, a tiny pool of water drew closer and closer. He shut his eyes and held his breath as he plunged beneath the surface. Evan went limp and let the water take him where it wanted. It pushed him left and pulled him right. Finally, his head bobbed up above the surface.

He gulped in a breath and wrapped his arms around his trombone case. It was soaked, but it still floated. Cleo and Gabriel, clutching flotation cushions, drifted alongside him, battered and bruised.

"You guys okay?" Gabriel coughed.

"Urrr," Teddy said. His usually fluffy fur lay matted against his body.

"'Urrr' for me, too," Cleo said.

Evan was too shaken to say anything, so he just nodded.

They drifted awhile, letting the sun bake their backs, until Evan felt something tugging on the fabric of his pants.

"What do you want, Cleo?"

"What do you mean what do I want?"

"Stop tugging on my pants."

"I'm not," she said. "My arms are busy grabbing this cushion. Anyhow, I've got better things to do than tug on your pants."

"I feel it, too," Gabriel said.

Suddenly, the water began bubbling and churning like they were in a gigantic hot tub. Something nibbled at Evan's legs and nipped his arm. He lifted his hand out of the water. Three oval-shaped fish hung from the sleeve of his shirt. They were mostly gray, with bright-red bellies. Their jaws pumped as they tried to bite, bite, bite!

"Piranhas!" Cleo screamed. "Get out of the water!"

"I said that a half hour ago!" Gabriel yelled. "Piranhas are eating machines!"

All three kids kicked toward the shore. Evan could feel the small fish grabbing at his

skin, at his clothes, at anything they could sink their teeth into. He, Cleo, and Gabriel swam like lightning until they landed on the muddy bank. Even in the shallow water, the piranhas kept biting, only disappearing when every part of every kid was on dry land.

Evan rolled onto his back, panting. His soaking wet trombone case lay beside him. But when he looked up, instead of blue sky, he saw yellow with purple polka dots.

Cleo clutched Evan's arm. "Locke's parachute."

CHAPTER 7

Aside from the sound of the waterfall in the distance, the jungle was silent. The parachute hung limply from some tree branches above them and swayed in the warm breeze.

"That's the last time I go rafting on the Amazon River," Gabriel said.

"Me too," Evan said. "But it *is* sort of beautiful . . ."

Cleo stood. "It's beautiful when the

animals aren't eating you and the rocks and waterfalls aren't pulverizing you."

"Good word," Evan said. "'Pulverize.'"

"Which way did Locke go?" Gabriel asked. They looked around the muddy bank.

Evan noticed some footprints in the mud. "Locke's boots. I can tell from the knobby treads."

"And look here," Gabriel added. "Some of these vines are cut. It seems like Locke bushwhacked his way through the jungle."

"What does 'bushwhacked' mean?" Evan asked.

"It means he cut through the jungle and made his own trail," Gabriel explained. "If you watched *Grizzly Romper*, you'd know that. Locke is probably following the tracking device."

Cleo tugged the parachute out of the branches. "Then that's the way we need to go."

"Urrr," Teddy said, hugging tightly to Cleo's back.

They made their way into the jungle. Branches arched over the trail, and so many vines hung down on either side, they looked like curtains. Although the sun was still high in the sky, it seemed dark. They followed Locke's path, which wound around huge trees and along tiny streams. Every so often one of the kids would think they had lost the trail, but then they'd spot knobby footprints in the mud or cut vines hanging down.

"Locke really covered a lot of ground," Evan said.

"It's that tracking device," Cleo said. "He knows exactly which way to go."

Gabriel took a sip of water that trickled from the end of a cut vine. "How do you know Locke?" he asked.

"We . . . uh . . . We don't," Cleo said.

"Then how do you know his name?" Gabriel said.

Evan scrambled to think of an excuse. "It was on his name tag," he said. "He had a gold name tag right on the chest of his uniform. Didn't you see it?"

Gabriel laughed. "I guess I was too busy almost falling out of the plane to notice."

Evan wanted to change the subject. "We sure have been through a lot in only a few hours."

"That's how survival stories go," Cleo said. "Full of danger and action."

"But this isn't a story," Gabriel said. "This is real life."

"Oh, of course," Cleo said. "As real as anything."

Gabriel gave Cleo a strange look, but she ignored it. They followed the trail until they came to a clearing. The ground was moist and soggy.

"Which way does the trail go?" Evan asked, looking around for footprints.

"I don't see any cut vines," Gabriel said.

They stood in the clearing for a few minutes, trying to decide what to do.

"Do these trees look like they're getting taller?" Cleo asked.

"No, but we're getting shorter," Evan said. "Look!"

While they had been trying to figure out which way to go, their feet had sunk into the soft ground up to their shins.

"Quicksand!" they all said at once.

Evan tried to pull one of his feet out, but the pressure just sucked his other leg in deeper. A big air bubble burped out of the ground, and they all began to sink more quickly.

"What do we do?" Cleo asked.

"You're the ones who watch *Grizzly Romper: Survive in the Wild*," Evan said. "What would Grizzly do?"

"Season two, episode six," Cleo said. "I missed that one."

"Hey, me too," Gabriel said. "What are the chances of that?"

"What are the chances we'll get out of this mess?" Evan said, tossing his trombone case onto dry land.

"I'd say none," a voice said from behind them.

Evan did his best to turn around, but it

was hard while he was standing up to his thighs in quicksand. "Locke!"

Locke walked around the edge of the quicksand, careful not to step into it. His mirrored sunglasses were cracked, and his pilot's jacket was torn. "When I found this quicksand pit, I knew I had to lure you here. You're the only ones who could spoil my plans to find that golden statue. If I stop you, I can take my time." He looked at the tracking device. "And that shouldn't be too hard. It's only about a mile away from here."

"Urrr," Teddy said.

"Traveling a mile through the thick jungle is harder than you think," Gabriel said. "We'll stop you."

"It's nice to see you're as brave as your two foolish friends," Locke said. "You can all sink together." He pointed to a rope that was tied around a tree trunk. "If only you could reach this. It's what I used to get across the quicksand safely. You could use it to pull yourselves out. What a shame it's so very far away . . ."

And with that, Locke turned around and disappeared into the jungle. They heard him laughing in the distance. Then they heard low howling. Two different howls.

"Glen and Gary," Cleo whispered. "I knew they were around here somewhere helping Locke."

"What do we do?" Evan said. By now, the quicksand was up to their hips.

Gabriel leaned forward, but he only sank faster. "If we could just reach that rope," he said.

"Hmm. Maybe we can," Cleo said. She

unwrapped Teddy's arms from her shoulders. "Can you get that rope for us, little guy?"

"Urrr."

Cleo tossed Teddy a few feet to the edge of the quicksand. He slowly rolled onto his belly and began to crawl. One arm reached forward, and then the other. One leg reached forward, and then the other.

"Urrr," Teddy said, as he pulled himself another few inches along the ground.

"Can't he go any faster?" Evan asked. The quicksand was already up past his belly button.

"He's a sloth," Cleo explained. "That *is* fast for him."

Teddy crawled along some more, his body slowly inching along the jungle floor.

"Come on, Teddy," Gabriel said. "You're going to have to speed things up."

Teddy looked over his shoulder at them. "Urrr."

"Don't distract him," Evan said. "It only slows him down."

"If he was going any slower, he'd be going backward," Gabriel said.

Teddy was almost at the rope. The trouble was that the quicksand was up to the kids' chests, and they were still sinking.

"Hurry, Teddy," Evan said.

"Urrr."

The quicksand crept toward their shoulders.

"Let's grab on to each other," Cleo said to the boys. "That way, if one of us gets pulled under at least we'll know where you are."

Teddy grabbed the end of the rope and put it in his teeth.

"Oh look, sloths' teeth look like people teeth," Cleo said, sinking to her neck. "That's so cute!"

"Save the observations for later," Gabriel said. "I don't think—"

But Gabriel's words got cut off as his face sank below the quicksand. Evan disappeared, too. The last thing Cleo saw before she vanished below the surface was Teddy crawling closer, the rope clenched in his very cute teeth.

Cleo pushed her hands above her head and reached up. The wet sand squeezed her and made it hard to move at all. It was impossible to breathe.

Suddenly, something fuzzy and warm touched her fingers. It was Teddy! Cleo grasped around and felt the rope against her palm. She grabbed it and began to pull.

Her body lurched upward, and Evan and Gabriel held onto her shoulders, climbing beside her. She used her other hand to pull harder. Before long, her head came out of the quicksand, and she gasped for air.

Teddy was smiling at her, his "people teeth" gleaming in the sun.

"Thank you, Teddy!" Cleo said.

"Urrr."

"Now let's get Evan and Gabriel out of that quicksand."

Cleo pulled Evan, and Evan pulled Gabriel. Teddy tried his best to pull all of them, but with his tiny body and tinier claws, it wasn't easy. Before long, they all lay on their backs, panting and wiping away the wet sand that covered them from head to toe.

"We've got to move along," Gabriel finally

said, rubbing grit from his eyes. "My parents trusted me with that statue. Plus, that tracker has a homing beacon. It's the only way we can signal our way out of the jungle. If we don't find it, we'll be stranded."

Evan agreed and stood up. They followed Locke's trail around giant rocks, through thick grass, and along a ravine. Finally, they came out of the jungle and found themselves on a rocky outcropping.

Cleo gasped in amazement.

In the distance, they saw a large, rust-colored mountain ridge. On top of the ridge sat the biggest tree any of them had ever seen. Its deep green branches were spread wide, like it was welcoming Evan, Cleo, and Gabriel. Beneath the tree were dozens of cave entrances.

"Why do I feel like we're going to have to go in one of those?" Evan asked, clutching his trombone case to his chest.

"Because that would make this a better story," Cleo answered as they headed straight for the cave.

CHAPTER 8

The cave was even spookier than Evan had imagined. Light shone in from a crack in the ceiling above, creating wide columns that made the rust-colored stone seem to glow. A small pile of bones sat in the center of the chamber. Dark nooks around the edge of the cavern had the kids' imaginations running wild about what could be hiding there, watching them.

"Urrr," Teddy said.

"Don't worry, little guy," Cleo reassured him. "I know you don't like caves. You live in trees."

Evan inspected the walls of the cavern. "Hey, look over here."

Cleo and Gabriel peered over his shoulder. On the wall of the cave someone had painted a handful of simple images.

"People," Cleo pointed out. "And trees."

"And over here," Gabriel said. "That looks like a horse, or maybe some kind of deer. My parents were right. We found the caves!"

Evan popped open his trombone case. Water dumped out, along with one flopping piranha. His trombone gleamed in a beam of sunlight. He pulled out a mostly dry sheet of music paper and a pen.

"What are you doing?" Cleo asked.

"I'm copying this art. It's possible no one

else has seen these cave paintings in a thousand years. We need evidence."

While Evan sketched the image of several hunters chasing a huge animal, Cleo looked at another section. "Look here," she said. "It's a drawing of a giant tree with a hollowed-out area underneath. It sort of looks like this mountain."

"The hollowed-out area is filled with people," Gabriel said. "My parents think humans lived in the deepest parts of the Amazon once. I wonder if they're right."

"Of course they are," Evan said. "Who do you think drew the paintings in the first place?"

Gabriel laughed. "I guess so."

"What are these animals?" Cleo asked Gabriel. "They have long tails and are hanging from the trees."

"They look like monkeys, don't you think?"

"There sure are a lot of them," Cleo said. "Why would anyone draw so many?"

"There are more over here," Evan said. "The artist must have really liked them."

Evan finished his copy of the cave painting. He folded the paper and placed it on top of his trombone in the case. He shut the lid and tried to lock the clasps. They kept popping back open. "It's broken," Evan said.

"Locke is still ahead of us," Gabriel said. "We need to move on. Leave the trombone behind."

"I can't," Evan said. "I need it."

He folded his sketch and stuffed it in his pocket. Then Evan removed the trombone from its case. He unhooked the case's strap and looped it through the brass tubing of the

89

trombone. He pulled the strap over one shoulder and stood up. The trombone hung at his side. "Okay, let's go."

The cave snaked deeper into the mountain. Sometimes the tunnel got so narrow they had to turn sideways to slide through or so low they had to crawl. Every time Evan's trombone scraped against the stone, he cringed. He would have to explain every little scratch to his mom and dad. The tunnel got darker and colder until Evan was sure they'd have to turn back.

Finally, Cleo, who was crawling ahead of him, gasped. "Amazing!" she whispered.

They inched out onto a ledge to see a huge cavern open in front of them. Thick vines and roots dangled from the ceiling. Ledges dotted with entrances to other tunnels lined the cavern and were only reachable by wooden ladders and a few rope bridges that looked too fragile to cross. Light streaming in from above shone on thousands of cave paintings covering the walls. A small fire burned at the far side of the cavern. Above it, a large painting of men and women dancing around a starburst flickered in the orange glow.

"It's totally amazing," Cleo said again.

"It's the archaeological find of a lifetime," Gabriel said.

Evan leaned close to Cleo. "It's the first magical library ever," he whispered.

Across the cavern, Locke was climbing a roughly made wooden ladder. Above him, on the topmost ledge, something glimmered in a beam of sunlight.

"The Golden Sloth!" Gabriel shouted.

"Urrr," Teddy said.

"You'll never catch me," Locke called out.

"I'll be the one to get that statue, and all the glory that comes with it!"

The kids leaped into action. Cleo and Gabriel hopped off the ledge and grabbed dangling vines. They swung side by side across the ancient cavern. Evan grabbed the railing of a rope bridge and carefully stepped out onto the first slat of wood. It creaked and wobbled under his foot.

"Are you nuts?" Cleo called over her shoulder as she swung to one of the wooden ladders. "That rope bridge looks like it's going to fall apart!"

"You know how I feel about heights," Evan said. "If I don't have to swing, I'm not swing—"

Just then, the wood snapped, and Evan dropped between the slats. He grabbed one of the ropes that held the bridge together, but it was old and frayed, and it ripped apart. In an instant, Evan was swinging, too. He slammed into the rock wall near Cleo, who grabbed him and pulled him onto the ledge.

"My parents discovered the Golden Sloth!" Gabriel shouted at Locke.

"You said it yourself. The first person to report a discovery is the one who gets credit for it. Anyhow, I only care about finding the silly statue because it will lead me to the next Jeweled Great."

The kids scrambled up a ladder to a higher ledge, but Locke was still far away and was getting closer to the Golden Sloth with each rung.

Evan knew there was no way they'd catch Locke by climbing. He looked around. "Hey, which one of us is the lightest?"

"Probably you," Cleo answered.

"I was afraid you'd say that."

"Why?" Gabriel asked.

Evan pointed to a hanging vine. It stretched high into the cavern and looped over a thick root. Both sides of the vine were just within reach. "If I grab one end and you two grab the other . . ."

Cleo grinned. "I thought you were scared of heights."

Evan smiled back. "I'd hate to see Locke get credit for the scientific discovery of a lifetime, you know. Credit should go to Gabriel's parents."

Evan wrapped one end of the vine around his forearm and held tight with his other hand. Gabriel and Cleo grabbed the other end.

"On the count of three," Gabriel said. "One . . . two . . ."

Evan shot into the air. "I thought you said on the count of three!" he cried out.

"We didn't want to give you a chance to chicken out!" Cleo hollered back. She and Gabriel plunged to the cavern floor as Evan rose higher.

Evan banged against the cavern walls. His trombone scraped along the rough surface. He passed Locke, who swiped at him with an open hand. Evan dodged and kept rocketing upward. When he reached the topmost ledge, Evan leaped onto it and unwrapped his arm. The Golden Sloth lay at his feet.

He bent down and picked it up. The tracking device on the side was still blinking.

That's when he saw them. Hundreds of howler monkeys hung from the vines and roots that dangled from the cavern ceiling.

And they looked angry.

CHAPTER 9

The monkeys began to hoot and growl.

"What do you want?" Evan asked.

One of the monkeys swung at Evan, who was so busy trying to keep his trombone from falling that he bobbled the Golden Sloth. The monkey snatched the statue from Evan's hands and tossed it to another monkey, who threw it to another. Before long, the Golden Sloth was being passed around like a hot potato.

Until Locke's hand shot up and grabbed the statue from the air.

"That's a good monkey," Locke said as he climbed onto Evan's ledge and dusted himself off. "Now all I have to do is activate the homing beacon and climb to the top of this mountain, and I'll be rescued." He leaned in close to Evan. "Rescued out of this horrible book."

Locke began to press buttons on the tiny keypad on the side of the statue. Nothing happened. "Oh, I'll figure it out once I get up there." He stuffed the Golden Sloth into his jacket and followed a narrow pathway that led to the crevice in the top of the cavern.

Evan could hear Locke laughing, which got the howler monkeys excited. They began to bellow their own calls.

BUUUUU—UUUUUUURRRRRRRP!

**HUUUURRR—RRRGGGGGHHHHH!
RAAAAA—WWWWWWWRRRKKK!**

The sounds were deafening, and Evan
had to cover his ears. By now, Cleo and
Gabriel had climbed up to the ledge and were
crouching at his side. They wanted to follow
Locke, but the monkeys closed in, blocking
their way. The hooting and hollering became
louder.

**HUUUURRR—RRRGGGGGHHHHH!
RAAAAA—WWWWWWWRRRKKK!**

One of the monkeys took a swipe at Cleo,
but she ducked.

Finally, Evan stood up. He lifted his trombone to his lips. The mouthpiece tasted like
muddy water and quicksand. Evan worried
that with all the dents in the brass he wouldn't
be able to make a sound. He took in a deep
breath, pursed his lips, and blew.

A glop of quicksand burped out of the horn.

He blew again.

WHOHHHHHHH-MMMMP!!!!

GHUUUUURRRRR-RRRRK!!!!!

The sound echoed off the walls. It even made Evan wince. The monkeys shrank back and began leaping excitedly from vine to vine.

"Keep tooting your horn!" Gabriel yelled over the sound of the trombone. "It's a sign of dominance. You're earning their respect!"

"You're not earning mine!" Cleo yelled, her hands pressed over her ears. "Let's get out of here!"

Evan continued to blow his trombone. It wasn't easy to keep up while running through a tunnel—he was used to sitting down while he played—but he did his best. The three of them ran along the path. As they made their way out onto the top of the mountain, Evan noticed a new drawing magically appearing on the wall of the cave. The dark red lines showed an image of three humans surrounded by monkeys. One of the humans was holding a long stick to his lips. Wait, it wasn't a stick; it was a curved horn! The three humans were them: Evan, Cleo, and Gabriel!

"Cleo, we're on the wall of the cave! I was right, this is a magical library!"

"We'll be splattered on the floor of this magical library if we don't get out of here!" Cleo said.

"Urrr," Teddy said from his perch on Cleo's back.

But a group of howler monkeys stood blocking their way. Glen and Gary crouched in front of the pack. The white fur around their faces was unmistakable.

"You need to come along with us if you want to go back," Evan said. "The end of the adventure—"

One of the white-faced monkeys shook its head.

"STAAAAAA-AAAYYYY." As it spoke, something moved in the monkey's arms. A baby howler monkey lifted its head and peeked at Evan with big, innocent eyes. It chirped out a tiny howl: "Erp!"

"They have family here," Cleo said. "They want to stay."

"STAAAAAA-AAAYYYY," the other monkey agreed.

Cleo looked at Evan. "Who are we to argue? They're better off here than with Locke."

"But they're monkeys," Evan said.

"Happy monkeys," Cleo said. "It's better than unhappy library assistants."

Evan, Cleo, and Gabriel ran out into the sunlight. The huge tree they had seen on top of the ridge loomed above them. Locke stood at the edge of the cliff, frantically pressing buttons on the statue.

"Drat! What is the code to activate the homing beacon?" he hollered.

"Guys." Gabriel pulled a folded paper from one of his shirt pockets. "I think I know the code."

The paper was soggy, but Evan recognized it. It was the letter from Gabriel's parents that had been packed in the box with the Golden Sloth.

"We have to get the statue from Locke first." Cleo pulled Teddy from her shoulders

and placed him on a low-hanging branch. "And I know just how to do that."

"How?" Gabriel asked.

"How do you catch flies?"

Evan made a sour face. "Who'd want to catch flies?"

"We've got these sticky traps around our research camp," Gabriel added.

"No, it's a figure of speech," Cleo said. "You catch them with honey. We have to be sweet to get what we want."

Cleo walked slowly toward Locke. "We think we know the code. If we work together, we can activate the rescue beacon and all be saved."

"In case you haven't figured it out yet, I'm not very big on teamwork," Locke grumbled. "Anyhow, if I enter the code myself, I can leave you miserable kids behind. The powers granted by finding all four Jeweled Greats will be mine alone."

Cleo realized sweetness wasn't going to work. She leaped at Locke, but he was ready. He stepped away and lifted the Golden Sloth over his head, out of Cleo's reach. She fell to the ground at his feet.

"You're not as clever or as fast as you think," Locke said.

"Maybe I'm more clever than you realize." Cleo saw movement in the branches above Locke. "And maybe it's not always being fast that counts."

Two brownish-gray, paws with long claws slowly reached down from a leafy branch and grabbed the Golden Sloth from Locke's hands.

"Urrr!" Teddy said from above. He dropped the statue to Cleo, who spun around and gave it a spinning kick. The Golden Sloth flew into the air and landed in Evan's hands.

Evan fumbled with the statue. "What's the code? What's the code?"

"It's my birthday," Gabriel said.

"Happy birthday," Evan said. "Strange time to mention it, though."

"No, the code for the homing signal *is* my birthday! If you read the uppercase letters in the note my parents left, it reads CODE YOUR BIRTHDAY. But I need to be the one to enter the numbers."

"I can do it," Evan said, knowing that he needed to key it in if they wanted to get back to their own magical library. By now, Locke was headed toward them.

Gabriel held out his hand. "I have to enter the code."

Locke was getting closer, but Gabriel didn't seem to care. Evan knew if Locke got the statue first, all hope would be lost. He handed the statue to Gabriel.

"My birthday is June twenty-eighth. That's zero-six-two-eight," he said, poking his finger at the keypad.

A red light blinked and a soft buzzer buzzed.

"Something's wrong." Gabriel typed in the code again.

The red light blinked brighter and the buzz got louder.

"Give me that!" Locke grabbed for the statue and knocked it from Gabriel's hands. It popped into the air and landed in Evan's arms.

He ran across the top of the mountain to Cleo, spun the statue around, and looked at the keypad. It looked like any other ten-digit keypad he had ever seen. Then he thought of something.

"I've got the answer," he said. "Remember that report I did on poison dart frogs?"

"I remember you telling me you did a report on them," Cleo said.

"You really don't remember when I talked ab—"

"I have to listen to you enough when we're in these books," Cleo said. "Anyhow, I was nervous about my own report."

"Cleo, nervous about something? I doubt it."

"I'm not very good at speaking in front of people."

Gabriel dodged Locke's grasping arms and rolled between his legs. Then he ran over to where Evan and Cleo were standing.

"Fear of public speaking?" Evan said. "But you seem really confident."

Cleo pointed at the statue. "I'd say we should talk less about me and more about that."

"Oh yeah," Evan said. "So, I read a bunch of magazine articles about poison dart frogs. Beautiful, brightly colored, and deadly. But something else I noticed in the articles is that in Brazil they don't do month first and then date. Here it's date first and then month."

"Let me do it!" Gabriel insisted.

"I've got it," Evan said.

He keyed in the numbers: two-eight-zero-six.

Letters burst from the Golden Sloth like a thousand crazy spiders. The letters tumbled in the air around them and began to spell words. The words became sentences, the sentences paragraphs. Something heavy and warm dropped into Cleo's arms. Cleo looked down, but couldn't see anything on account of the swirling words. Before long, they could barely see through the letter confetti, and then everything went black.

CHAPTER 10

They were back in their school clothes, and the magical library was just as they had left it, with a few rather large exceptions.

The first thing they noticed was the greenery. A huge Amazonian tree grew in the corner of the library. Its branches spread across the ceiling. Roots cropped up from the floor, creating curved and knotty benches and tables. Vines hung down that could be used to climb to the library's uppermost walkways. Walkways Evan and Cleo had never been able to reach before.

"Urrr," Teddy said. He was snuggled in Cleo's arms, looking quite ready for a nap. Cleo lifted him onto a branch, and he grabbed it with his clawed hands and feet. Within moments, Teddy was headed to the higher parts of the library tree at his very slow, Teddy-like pace. He looked at Cleo and smiled.

"Awww, people teeth," she said.

Evan's trombone case sat on one of the new tables. It sparkled as though it were brand-new. Evan popped it open to find his trombone gleaming inside—the brass unmarred and undented.

Evan sighed in relief. "Mr. Oinks can stay full."

"Well, I've never seen anything like this before," a voice said from behind them.

"Gabriel!" Cleo said. "How did you get here?"

"I had a feeling there was something special about you two." He reached into the collar of his shirt and pulled out a necklace. A silver pendant that looked like a key hung from it.

Evan held his hand to his chest. Under his sweater, he felt his own key pendant—the one that meant they were honorary librarians and Key Hunters. "It's just like ours."

"I don't really live in Brazil," Gabriel explained. "I live in New York City. My magic library is in Manhattan. You didn't think you were the only Key Hunters out there, did you?"

"We're sort of figuring this whole thing out as we go along," Evan said.

"So how did you end up in our adventure?" Cleo asked Gabriel.

"I should ask you the same question," Gabriel said. "I'm sort of new to this as well, but I'll tell you what I know." He swept his arm around and gestured at all the books in the library. "These books are gateways from one magical world to another. They are all here for us to explore, just like the real world is. Because after all, we're all heroes in our own stories, right?"

"Well, I can tell you something is definitely going wrong in our story," Cleo said. "Our library is changed. That tree, these benches . . ."

Gabriel ran his hand along one of the new

tables. "You're right. Something is wrong. We should never have been in the same book at the same time."

"Locke forced his way into our version of *Quest for the Lost Sloth*," Evan suggested.

Gabriel thought for a moment. "Of course—Locke broke one of the basic rules of the library: Only enter a book when you are ready for it . . . and only when the book is ready for you."

The sound of shuffling feet came from a balcony above them. "Everything would have been fine if it weren't for you three getting in my way," Locke growled. "Now we're back outside the book with no Jeweled Great to speak of."

"I'm not so sure about that," Evan said.

He reached into his pocket and pulled out the sketch of the cave art he had drawn. The paper was soggy and sloppy, but Evan could make out the hunters with spears chasing the deer. He placed it on the second pedestal, which began to glow. A burst of light flashed, and glitter rained down. There, sitting on the pedestal, sat a flat, reddish stone with rust-colored figures on it: hunters chasing a deer.

"It's not the original," Evan said.

"But it's a perfect copy," Cleo said. "The magical library seems to like it. I think we've found the second Jeweled Great."

"It may not be covered in diamonds or rubies, but it's a jewel of history," Evan said.

"Very well," Locke said. "But tomorrow I'm leading the adventure. All three of you will do exactly as I say."

Evan felt the homing beacon buzz in his front pocket. Even though it was electronic, he knew this had to be the next key. "I'm sorry, Locke," he said. "Our plans have changed."

"We need the last two Jeweled Greats!" Locke screamed. "Your plans have not changed!"

"Of course they have," Cleo said. "We need to find a way to get Gabriel home."

And with that, all three of them—Evan, Cleo, and Gabriel—grabbed the nearest vine and began to climb.

The Lost Library is full of exciting—and dangerous—books! And Evan and Cleo have a magical key to open one of them. Where will they end up next? Read on for a sneak peek of *Battle of the Bots*!

"Where are we?" Cleo asked.

Evan reached toward a window and pulled aside the curtain. Although there were some strange, modern buildings out there, Evan recognized the skyline. "I think we're in a weird future version of New York City. That's the Chrysler Building over there."

"It's called the Usmanov Building now."

Gabriel zipped out of the bedroom on what looked like an electric wheelchair. But there were no wheels on it—the chair floated a few inches above the ground.

"Years ago, a wealthy businessman bought the Chrysler Building and renamed it," he explained, adjusting the high-tech blue head-band he wore. "I'm happy to be safely out of our last adventure, but less happy to be home."

"Hey Gabriel . . ." Cleo began shyly. "In

the book about the Amazon, even in our own library, you were able to . . ."

"To walk?" Gabriel said. "That's the magic of fiction. In my real world—this world—I use a hoverchair. This one hides all sorts of tricks. I upgraded it myself."

"So how did you know we needed to plug into that laptop to get here?" Cleo asked.

Gabriel pulled his own laptop out of a pocket on the side of his hoverchair. It had a sticker on it of a fist wrapped in thorny vines holding a lightning bolt. It was the same one from their magic library. "I had a hunch," he said.

"Well, since this is your world, what are we supposed to do in this story?" Evan asked.

Gabriel put one finger over his lips, and pointed to the door. He floated into the dim hallway and glided around a corner. Cleo put on her backpack, then she and Evan followed Gabriel to an old elevator. They took it to the top floor of the apartment building and went onto the roof.

"Whoa," Cleo said. "The view is much better out here."

Drones zipped in every direction. Sleek luxury ships cruised along the nearby river. Sunlight gleamed off glass skyscrapers that reached higher than any building Evan had ever seen. Above it all, a giant, silver blimp loomed in the sky.

"Even here we must be quiet," Gabriel explained. "They are always watching, always listening."

"Who is?" Evan asked.

"The Network."